The DANCING SKELETON

by Cynthia C. DeFelice
illustrated by Robert Andrew Parker

ALADDIN PAPERBACKS

FOR BUNNY AND GRAM — C.C.DeF.

FOR MAX — R.A.P.

First Aladdin Paperbacks edition September 1996

Aladdin Paperbacks
An imprint of Simon & Schuster
Children's Publishing Division
1230 Avenue of the Americas
New York, NY 10020

The text of this book was set in 15-point Cochin.
The illustrations were rendered in pen-and-ink and watercolor.

Printed in Hong Kong

10 9 8 7 6 5 4 3 2 1

The Library of Congress has cataloged the hardcover edition as follows:
DeFelice, Cynthia C.
The dancing skeleton / by Cynthia C. DeFelice ; illustrated by Robert Andrew Parker —
1st American ed.
p.   cm.
Summary: An ornery dead man refuses to stay in his coffin and causes a disturbance
when the best fiddler in town comes to call on his widow.
ISBN 0-02-726452-1
[1. Folklore — United States.]   I. Parker, Robert Andrew, ill.   II. Title.
PZ8.1.D3784Dan   1989
398.2'1'0973 — dc19   [E]   88-30245

ISBN 0-689-80453-9 (Aladdin pbk.)

Aaron Kelly was dead.

There wasn't anything anybody could do about it.
And, to tell you the truth, nobody much cared.
Aaron had been so downright mean and ornery in his life
that folks were glad to see him go.

Even his widow never shed a tear.

She just bought a coffin, put Aaron in it, and buried him.

Good-bye, Aaron Kelly, and good riddance!

But that very night, Aaron got up out of his grave,
walked through the graveyard, and came home.

His widow was sitting in the parlor,
thinking how peaceful and quiet it was without Aaron around,
when he walked right in the door.

"What's all this?" he shouted.
"You're all dressed in black. You look like somebody died.
Who's dead?"

The widow pointed a shaking finger at Aaron.
"You are!" she said.

"Oh, no, I ain't!" hollered Aaron.
"I don't feel dead. I feel fine!"

"Well, you don't look fine," said the widow.
"You look dead! Now you just get yourself
back in that coffin where you belong."

"Oh, no," said Aaron.
"I ain't goin' back to that coffin
till I feel dead."

Just plain ornery, he was.

Well, since Aaron wouldn't go back to the grave,
his widow couldn't collect the life insurance.
Without that money, she couldn't pay for the coffin.
If she didn't pay for the coffin,
the undertaker might take it back.
And if he did that, she'd *never* be rid of Aaron!

Aaron didn't care.

He just sat in his favorite rocking chair,

rocking back and forth,

     back and forth,

     day after day,

     night after night.

But after a while, Aaron began to dry up.
Pretty soon he was nothing but a skeleton.
Every time he rocked, his old bones clicked and clacked.
His widow did her best to ignore him,
but it wasn't easy with all the racket he made.

Then one night, the best fiddler in town
came to call on Aaron's widow.
He'd heard Aaron was dead,
and he thought he might marry that woman himself.

The fiddler and the widow sat down together,
cozylike, on the bench...
...and ole Aaron sat right across from them,
just a-creakin' and a-crackin' and a-grinnin'.

Fiddler said, "Woman,
how long am I going to have to put up
with that old bag o' bones sitting there?
I can't court you proper
with him staring at me like that!"

Widow answered, "I know! But what can we do?"

The fiddler shrugged.
The widow sighed.
The clock ticked.
And Aaron rocked.

Finally, Aaron said, "Well, *this* ain't any fun at all.
Fiddler, take out your fiddle. I feel like dancin'!"

So the fiddler took out his fiddle and he began to play.
My, my! He could make that fiddle sing!

Aaron Kelly heard that sweet music and he couldn't sit still.
He stood up. Oooh, his dry bones felt stiff!
He stretched himself.
He shook himself.
He cracked his knucklebones — aaah!
And he began to dance.

With his toe bones a-tappin'
and his feet bones a-flappin',
round and round he danced like a fool!
With his finger bones a-snappin'
and his arm bones a-clappin',
how that dead man did dance!

The music grew wilder, and so did Aaron
until, suddenly, a bone broke loose from that dancing skeleton,
flew through the air,
and landed on the floor with a C L A T T E R !

"Oh, my!" cried the fiddler. "Look at that!
He's dancing so hard, he's *falling apart!*"

"Well, then," said the widow, *"play faster!"*

The fiddler played faster.

Bones began flying every whichway,
and still that skeleton danced!

"Play louder!" cried the widow.

The fiddler hung on to that fiddle.
He fiddled a tune that made the popcorn pop.
He fiddled a tune that made the bedbugs hop.
He fiddled a tune that made the rocks get up and dance!

Crickety-crack, down and back!
Old Aaron went a-hoppin',
his dry bones a-poppin'.
Flippin' and floppin',
they just kept droppin'!

Soon there was nothing left of Aaron
but a pile of bones lying still on the floor...

...all except for his old bald head bone,
and *that* looked up at the fiddler,
snapped its yellow teeth, and said,
"O O O O O W E E E E ! AIN'T WE HAVIN' FUN!"

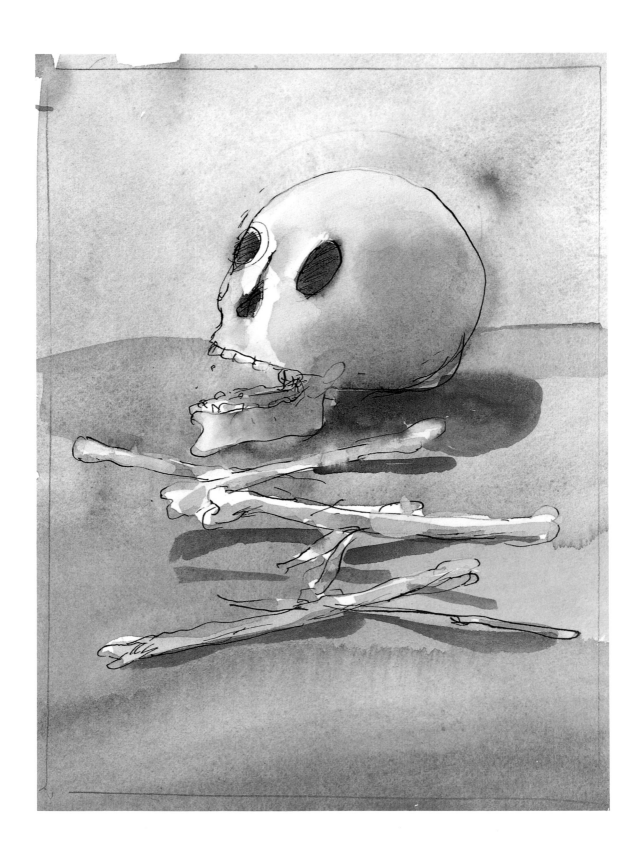

It was all too much for the fiddler.
He dropped his fiddle,
said, "Woman, I'm getting out of here!"
and ran out the door.

The widow gathered up Aaron's bones
and carried them back to the graveyard.
She put them in the coffin
and mixed them all around in there,
so Aaron could never put himself back together.

After that, Aaron Kelly stayed in his grave
where he belonged.

But folks say that if you walk by the graveyard
on a still summer night when the crickets are fiddling their tunes,
you'll hear a faint clicking and clacking down under the ground.
And you'll know...
it's Aaron's bones,
still trying to dance.

And what about the fiddler and the widow?
Well, they never did get together again.

Aaron Kelly had made DEAD SURE of that!

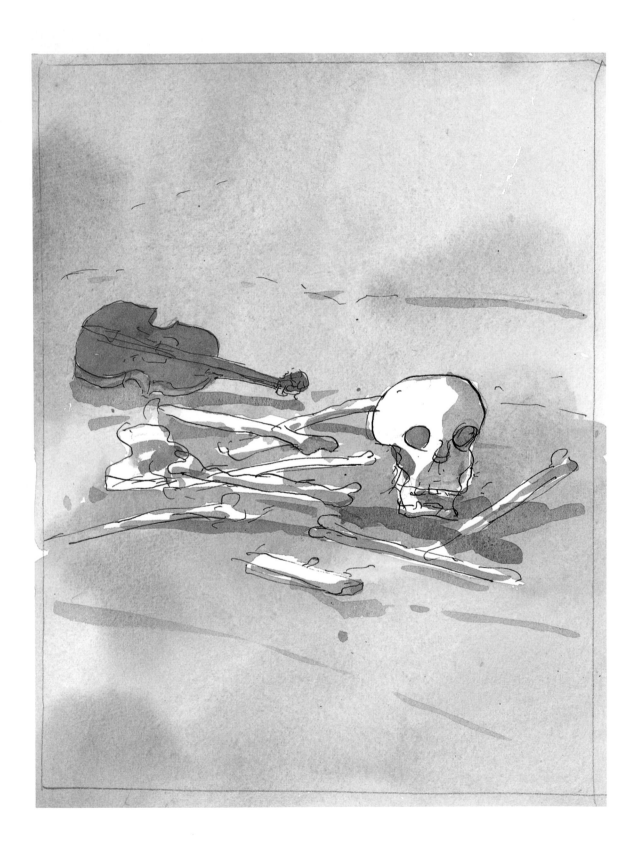